My Zoo Animals

Activity and Sticker Book

BLOOMSBURY
Activity Books

NEW YORK LONDON NEW DELHI SYDNEY

Can you find the panda
hidden in the picture?

2

3

Color the patterns on the snakes.

Find some fish stickers
to add to the aquarium.

6

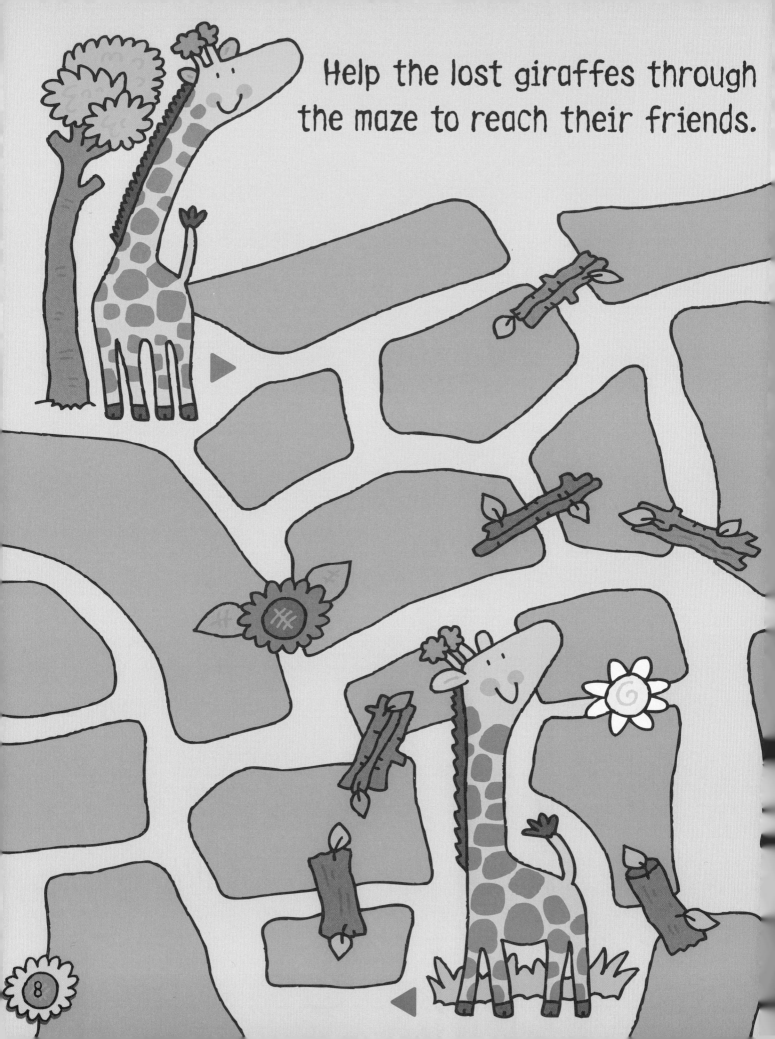

Help the lost giraffes through the maze to reach their friends.

Color in the crocodiles.

Find some monkey stickers to add to the picture.

How many rabbits, guinea pigs, sheep, and goats are in Pets' Corner?

Find the sticker signs to add to their huts and pen.

Spot the differences between the 2 elephant

pictures. There are 8 to find.

Can you find some stickers

to add to the big cat area?

Count the penguins. Give some of them hat or bow tie stickers.

Can you find some fish stickers
to feed to them?

Can you spot the zebra that is different?

Can you count 9 purple feathers

24

in the parrot cage?

Which balloon belongs to which meerkat?
Follow the strings to find out.

Draw lines between the matching

pairs in the reptile house.

Search the picture and find 5 butterflies,

4 spiders, 3 beetles, 2 snails, and a toucan.

Find the stickers to match the shapes.